A GOLDEN BOOK • NEW YORK

BARBIE and associated trademarks and trade dress are owned by, and used under license from, Mattel, Inc.
© Copyright 2004 Mattel, Inc. All Rights Reserved.
Published in the United States by Golden Books, an imprint of Random House Children's Books,
a division of Random House, Inc., New York, and simultaneously in Canada by Random House
of Canada Limited, Toronto. No part of this book may be reproduced or copied in any form
without written permission from the copyright owner. Golden Books, A Golden Book, and
the G colophon are registered trademarks of Random House, Inc.
Library of Congress Control Number: 2003105376   ISBN: 0-375-82727-7
www.goldenbooks.com
PRINTED IN CHINA   10 9 8 7 6 5 4 3 2 1

STARRING Barbie #3

The Belle of the Ball

By Alison Inches
Illustrated by Karen Wolcott

Cover photography by Joe Dias, Shirley Ushirogata, Bill Coutts, Greg Roccia, Lisa Collins, and Judy Tsuno

"Hi!" says Barbie. "You're just in time for the shoot of my very first romance, *The Belle of the Ball*. In this movie, I play a Southern farm girl who lives next door to a wealthy landowner and his handsome son, Jake Wilcox.

My character really wants to be a Southern belle—someone who is charming, proper, and wealthy, and wears great clothes!"

"Places, everyone!" calls the director.

"Well, I'd better get going!" says Barbie. "I hope you enjoy the movie."

In the Deep South, a beautiful girl named Anna Bradford dreams of becoming a Southern belle so that she can capture the heart of her neighbor Jake Wilcox.

But Anna needs to help out on the family farm. She feeds the chickens, milks the cows, and churns the butter.

"Butterfingers!" says Anna, laughing as she gets butter all over her hands.

Every day Anna watches Jake ride his horse on the grounds of the large manor next door.

"He is the handsomest man alive!" Anna says. "But he'd probably never be interested in me—especially in these clothes."

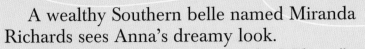

A wealthy Southern belle named Miranda Richards sees Anna's dreamy look.

"Don't get any ideas about Jake Wilcox," says Miranda as she passes by in her carriage. "He'll never notice a common girl like you!"

Anna is hurt by Miranda's words, but she does her best to ignore them.

The next day, Anna's mother asks her
to deliver some curtains she has made for
Mrs. Wilcox's parlor.

As Anna walks up to the Wilcox mansion, she sees Miranda and her friends sipping lemonade on the veranda.

"What on earth is *she* doing here?" Miranda asks her friends.

"Thank you, Anna," says Mrs. Wilcox. "I hope you can come to our cotillion next week," she adds as she hands Anna an invitation.

"It would be an honor to attend," says Anna with a curtsy.

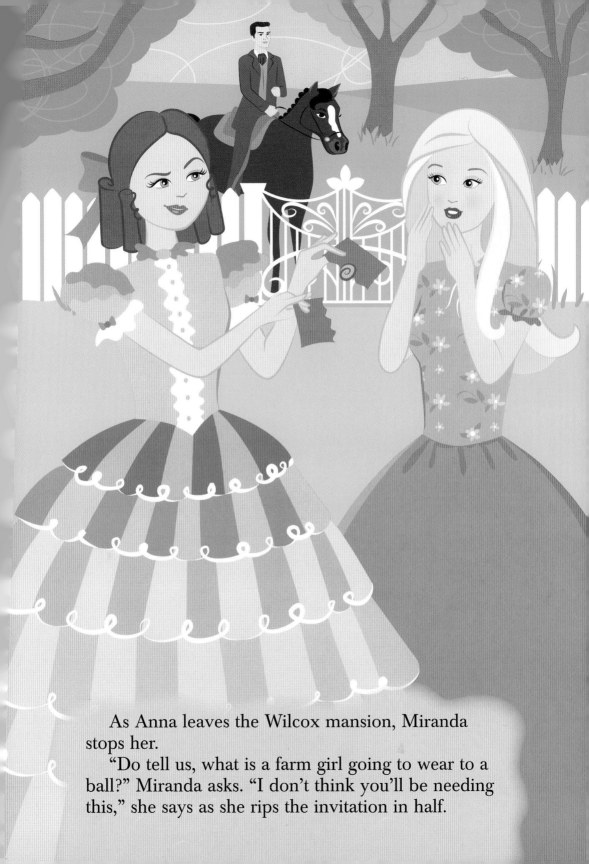

As Anna leaves the Wilcox mansion, Miranda stops her.

"Do tell us, what is a farm girl going to wear to a ball?" Miranda asks. "I don't think you'll be needing this," she says as she rips the invitation in half.

Anna is so upset that she hurries back to
her house in tears. Suddenly, there is a knock
at the door. It's Jake Wilcox!

"I saw what happened back at the manor,"
Jake says. "Miranda had no right to tear up
your invitation. I hope you'll come to the ball
as my special guest."

"Oh, thank you," Anna says with a smile.

Later, Anna tells her mother that Jake has invited her to the ball.

"Then we'll just have to make you the most beautiful dress in the South!" declares her mother. "I've been saving these for you," she says as she pulls out gorgeous satin, lace, and organza from her sewing trunk.

"Oh, Mother!" exclaims Anna.

When she is not doing chores, Anna designs a beautiful cotillion dress with petticoats, lace, and ruffles. Her mother takes the pattern and sews the dress.

"You look stunning, Anna!" says her mother.

On the night of the ball, the guests can't take
their eyes off Anna as she makes her grand entrance.
"Who is that?" Miranda asks her friends.
"What a glamorous gown!" others whisper.

But nobody finds Anna more beautiful than
Jake Wilcox. He doesn't leave her side all night.

"It was so kind of you to invite me tonight," Anna says as she and Jake twirl across the floor.

"I've wanted to dance with you for a long time," says Jake. "I've watched you working on your farm and in your garden. You are so lovely and sweet. And you make everything look like fun."

"I'm falling in love with you," Jake says.
Anna melts into Jake's arms.

"I love you, too!" Anna whispers.
As they embrace, the guests clap and cheer.

"Cut!" calls the director. "That's a take!"
"I always like happy endings," says Barbie.
"And I hope you liked *The Belle of the Ball*.
See you at my next movie!"

Here are some great Barbie™ storybooks to collect!

STARRING BARBIE™ SERIES

BARBIE™ DIRECT-TO-VIDEO SERIES

BARBIE™ RULES SERIES

A WEDDING BOOK

BARBIE™ LITTLE GOLDEN BOOKS®